This book
belongs to:

_____

MESSAGE TO PARENTS

This book is perfect for parents and children to read aloud together. First read the story to your child. When you read it again, run your finger under each line, stopping at each picture for your child to "read." Help your child to figure out the picture. If your child makes a mistake, be encouraging as you say the right word. Point out the written word beneath each picture in the margin on the page. Soon your child will be "reading" aloud with you, and at the same time learning the symbols that stand for words.

Library of Congress Cataloging-in-Publication Data

Slier, Debby.
    The Brementown musicians / retold by Debby Slier : illustrated by Heidi Petach.
       p. cm. — (A Read along with me book)
    Summary: Retells the classic tale in a rebus format.
    ISBN 0-02-898239-8
    [1. Fairy tales. 2. Folklore—Germany. 3. Rebuses.] I. Petach, Heidi. ill. II. Title. III. Series.
PZ8.S394Br 1989
398.2'452'0943—dc19
[E]   89-588
                                                                   CIP
                                                                   AC

The Brementown Musicians

A Read Along With Me Book

Retold by **Debby Slier**
Illustrated by **Heidi Petach**

 **CHECKERBOARD PRESS**
NEW YORK

donkey

One day, an old  who could no longer work heard his master making plans to be rid of him. The  , fearing for his life, decided to run away to Bremen. "There I will be a musician," he said.

As the walked along the he met a who looked very sad.

"Why so sad, ?" asked the .

"Woe is me," said the . "Now that I am too old to hunt, my master wants me dead. So I must run away. But I do not know how I shall earn my ."

"Come with me to Bremen,"

road

dog

bread

donkey

dog

road

cat

said the . "There we will work as musicians."

The agreed to go with the and they walked along the together. Before long they met a sad-looking .

"Why so sad, ?" asked the .

"Ah, me," said the . "Now that I am old and can no longer catch mice, my mistress wants to

be rid of me. So now I must find a

new home."

"Come with us," said the .

"We are going to Bremen to be

musicians. You can sing along

with us."

cat

donkey

dog

three

road

rooster

So the joined the

and the . And the

traveled along the together.

Before long they came to a

farmyard where a was

crowing loudly.

" , why do you crow so

loudly?" asked the  .

"Because I am old and no longer please my mistress. She has told the cook to make soup of me," replied the .

"Come with us to Bremen," said the . "You can join our band of musicians."

The agreed to go. So the animals continued down the .

By nightfall they were still far

woods

tree

donkey

dog

from Bremen. They decided to spend the night in the and stopped beside a large . The and the lay down beneath the . The

and the chose the

branches. The flew to the

top of the . From there

he saw a light shining from a

distant .

"Well, look at that," said the

 . "A  would be a better

place to spend the night."

So the  , the , the

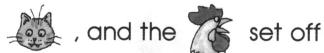 , and the set off

toward the .

animals

house

window

table

food

cat

When the got to the

they all looked in at the .

There they saw a band of robbers

sitting at a covered with the

most delicious .

"This is a good for us," said

the . "But first we must get

rid of the robbers. I have a plan."

At a given signal from the ,

the brayed, the

barked, the crowed, and the

 meowed.

And at the same instant all the

 smashed through the !

The robbers were so frightened

that they rushed out of the .

The friends then sat down

and ate the on the .

donkey

dog

rooster

four

donkey

straw

dog

door

cat

When they had finished eating,

each chose a sleeping place.

The lay down on a pile of

 . The curled up beside

the . The  found a warm

place by the . And the

 flew up and settled in a

comfortable spot beneath the

rafters. Then the  blew out

the .

From the , the robbers

watched the . When all was

quiet and dark, their chief said,

"It was only the wind that made

all that noise. Now it has blown

out the ."

house

cat

fire

Then the robber chief sent the

youngest robber back to the

 to make sure that it really

was safe for them to return.

The young robber went first to

the kitchen. Thinking the eyes of the

 were the , he tried to

kindle a light. But the spat

and scratched him. He tried to run

away, but the at the

bit him on the . And as he

ran the  kicked him. The ,

awakened by all the noise, let out

a loud "cock-a-doodle-doo!"

The terrified robber ran as

quickly as he could back to his

friends.

"A most terrible witch is now

in the house," he said. "She

leg

house

four

scratched me with her long nails, and when I tried to run away she stabbed me on the . Next she hit me with a club. And as I ran she let out a most terrible scream. I came away as fast as I could."

The robbers were now too afraid to go back to the . "Let's find a with peace and quiet," said the chief robber. And the friends?

They happily lived out their days in the in the . And they were so comfortable there that they never went to Bremen to be musicians.

woods

Words I can read

☐ animals   ☐ food   ☐ three
☐ bread   ☐ four   ☐ tree
☐ candle   ☐ house   ☐ window
☐ cat   ☐ leg   ☐ woods
☐ dog   ☐ road
☐ donkey   ☐ rooster
☐ door   ☐ straw
☐ fire   ☐ table